DOTTI

Tall Tale

Written by

Vicky Phillips

Illustrated by

Shey Kolee

For Freddie, whose arrival filled our world with joy – at the same time as this book found its way into the world.

May you grow up surrounded by stories and enjoy finding magic and new adventures on every page.

Down by the sea,
Where a little town lay,
Lived a girl named Dottie,
Who loved to play.

Dottie made up stories,
As wild as could be,
But these fibs hid a secret,
Which others could see.

When playing with friends,
She would often lie,
“That’s just not true!”
The others would cry.

“It happened! It did!
I’m telling the truth,
My mum’s been an explorer,
Since her youth.”

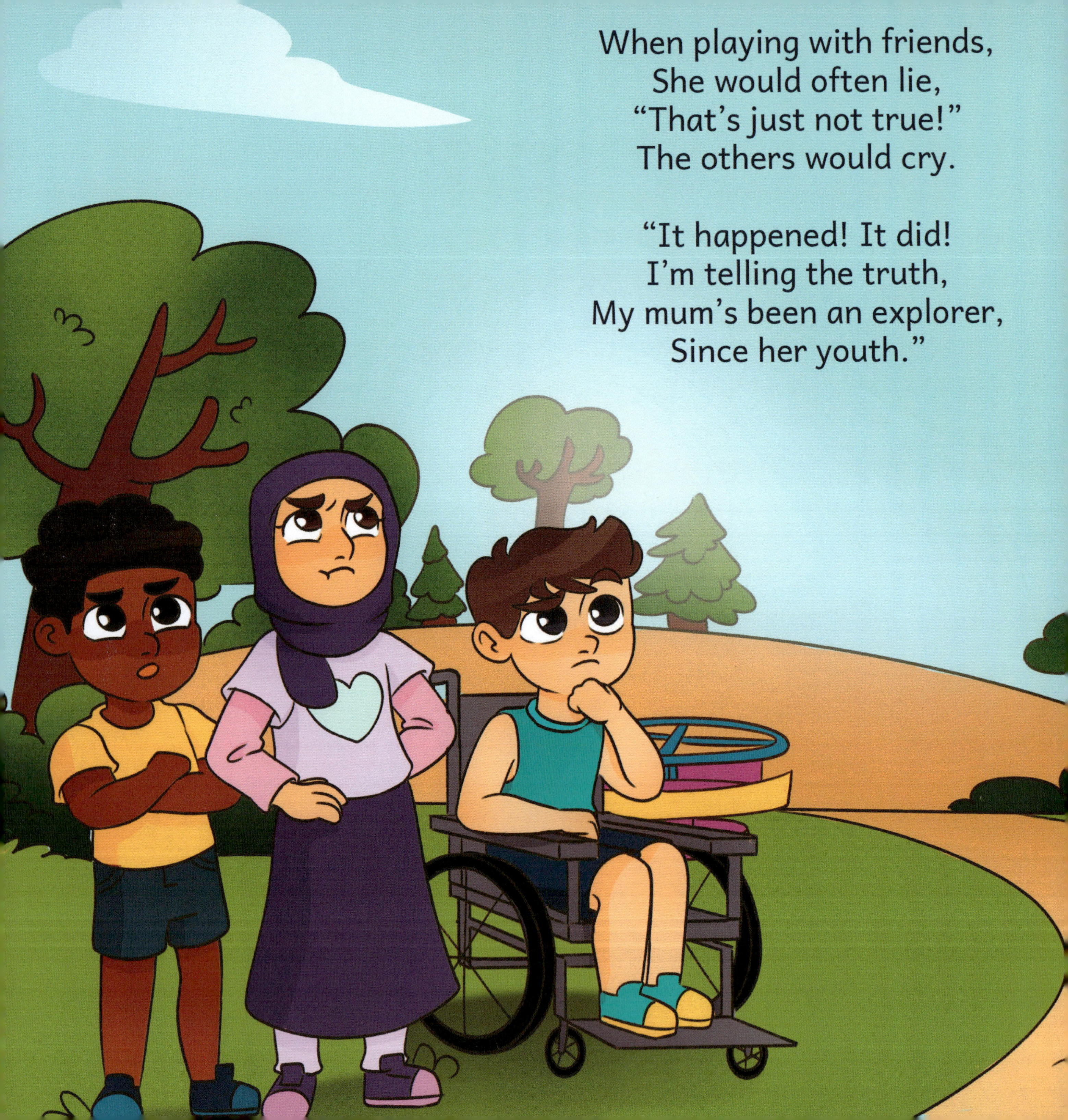

"Please stop it, Dottie,
There's just no need,
To make up stories,"
The children did plead.

When Dottie turned six,
She began to tell tales,
Like her mum was at sea,
Away saving the whales.

When her friends' mums were there,
It was hard to ignore,
That Dottie's mum disappeared,
When she'd just turned four.

“You won’t see her today,”
The young girl exclaimed,
“She’s away catching a lion,
That cannot be tamed.

Oh yes, it’s true,
You’ll believe me soon,
My Mum’s out in the wild,
But she’s due back in June.”

“Please stop it, Dottie,
There’s just no need,
To make up stories,”
The children did plead.

A few days later,
When out at the park,
"What's the lie today?"
Rude Ralph did remark.

She needed a new plan,
To convince all the boys,
"She's busy, okay!"
She screamed over the noise.

"She was driving a sports car,
Like she always does,
When up from the sky,
She heard a huge buzz.

Then one thousand bees,
Flew down into her car,
And with all that commotion,
She couldn't drive far!"

“Please stop it, Dottie,
There’s just no need,
To make up stories,”
The children did plead.

One day, in Art class,
Dottie painted a scene.
“It’s my mother,” she declared,
“This shows just where she’s been.”

The picture was grand,
A lady dressed all in red,
With a sparkling crown,
Perched on top of her head.

"She's on the red carpet, at a movie premier,
Hollywood's next big star, crowds all gather and cheer.

She's in a new film, making oh so much money,
She's the lead role, you know, and it's terribly funny."

"Please stop it, Dottie, there's just no need,
To make up stories," the children did plead.

As Dottie grew older,
Her stories progressed,
But her friends and her teachers,
Were never impressed.

"This time it's true,
She's really gone far,
She sped off in a rocket,
Flying right past a star!

They launched just last week,
And she's gone for a year,
She'll bring back some moon rocks,
As a souvenir."

The children all sighed,
Whilst rolling their eyes,
For they knew that young Dottie,
Was making up lies.

"Please stop it, Dottie,
There's just no need,
To make up stories,"
The children did plead.

They all knew she was lying,
But couldn't think why,
'I know,' Dottie thought,
'I'll say she's a spy!'

"She's away on a mission,
Top secret, you know,
I heard she's in Canada,
Camping out in the snow.

She's lying in wait,
'Til they catch the bad guy,
Then she'll hop on a plane,
And parachute out from the sky!

That's how she escapes,
After completing a mission,
Then she'll appear back at home,
Just like a magician."

“Please stop it, Dottie,
There’s just no need,
To make up stories,”
The children did plead.

A few years had gone past, and still no one knew,
Then one day a new woman showed up, out of the blue.

"Dottie, my darling, time to come home for tea."
Dottie turned and she fled, as fast as could be.

"Who was that old lady?"
Asked the children confused.
"It can't be her mother,"
Said Rude Ralph bemused.

“She said she was young,
With curly, long hair,
But that lady’s ancient,
With wrinkles everywhere!”

“Please stop it, Dottie,
There’s just no need,
To make up stories,”
The children did plead.

Her secret was out,
There was no hiding it now,
She'd have to come clean,
About her home life somehow.

The next day at school,
With great courage she mustered,
Tried to explain to her friends,
But got rather flustered.

"You see...my Mum..."
She began with a forced smile,
"Has been out of the picture,
And away for a while.

I don't know where, or exactly why,
But I've been being fostered,"
She began to cry.

"Please stop it, Dottie, there's just no need,
You're loved by us all!" the children agreed.

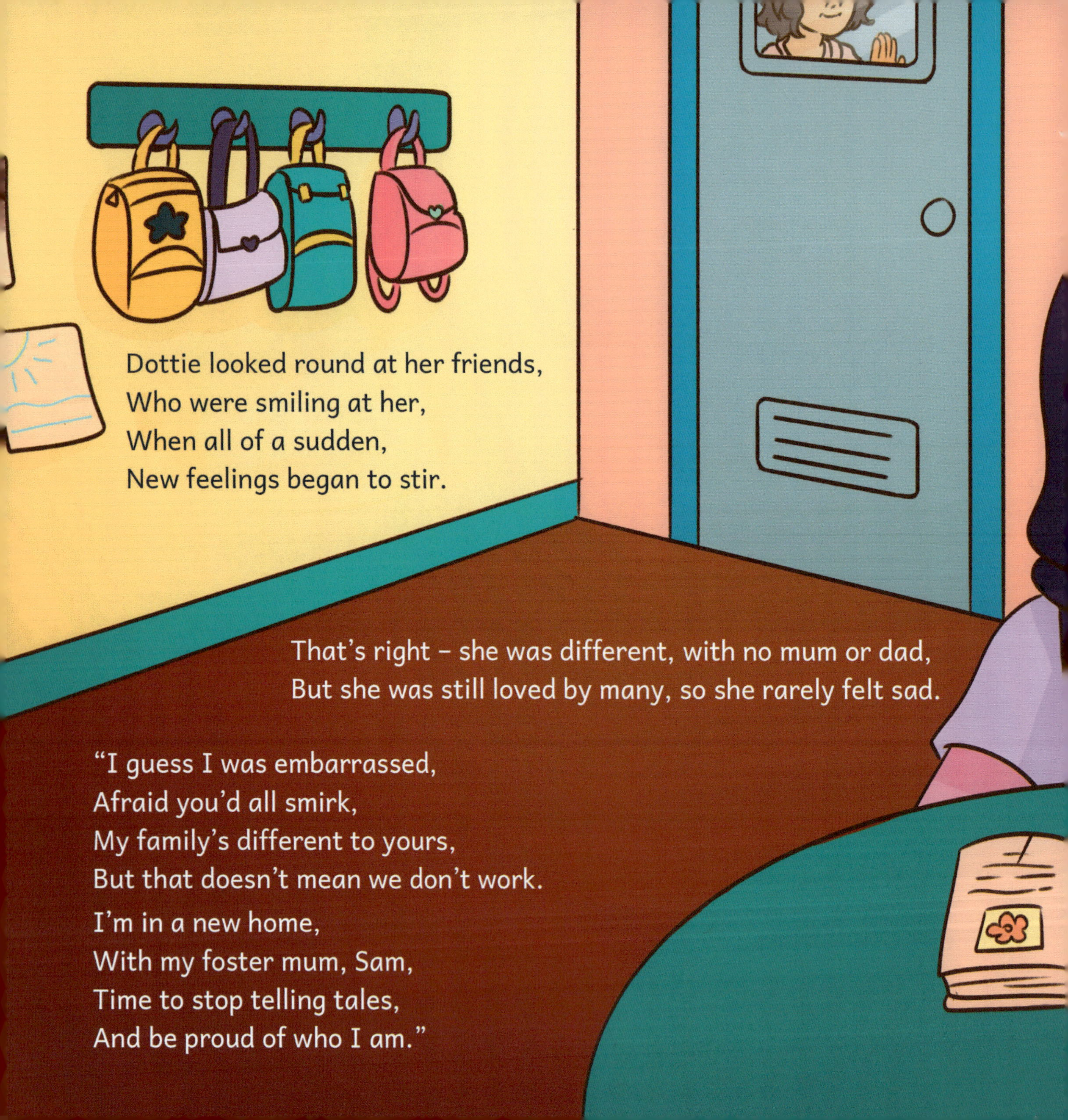

Dottie looked round at her friends,
Who were smiling at her,
When all of a sudden,
New feelings began to stir.

That's right – she was different, with no mum or dad,
But she was still loved by many, so she rarely felt sad.

"I guess I was embarrassed,
Afraid you'd all smirk,
My family's different to yours,
But that doesn't mean we don't work.

I'm in a new home,
With my foster mum, Sam,
Time to stop telling tales,
And be proud of who I am."

“That’s right, Dottie,
Don’t feel ashamed of your past,
But can you still tell us stories...?”
They cheekily asked.

Mouse Hunt

Dottie has a special friend—a tiny mouse—who loves to join in her adventures! This little mouse is always sneaky, hiding in different places throughout the story. Can you spot where he is hiding in each scene?

As you read through the pages, keep your eyes peeled and see if you can find him in every picture. He might be behind a tree, peeking from a window, or even sitting on a shelf. Sometimes, he might be with a friend who is also trying to stay out of sight!

Have fun looking for these miniature surprises and see how many mice you can find. Ready, set, go—let the mouse hunt begin!

What is Fostering?

In this book, we discover that Dottie is being fostered. Just like Dottie, there are lots of children across the world who live with foster families. These families give children a safe and happy place to stay while their own family might not be able to look after them. Fostering is an important way to make sure children feel safe and happy, even if things aren't going quite how they imagined.

Children may need fostering for many reasons. Sometimes their parents can't look after them due to illness or other challenges, and they need a safe place to stay until things get better. The family a child stays with during this time is known as the foster family. They take care of the child, making sure they feel happy and safe. Some children stay for a short time, while others may stay for longer, depending on their situation and the support their family needs.

Foster parents can offer a warm and caring environment to help children feel secure. In some cases, when things don't improve, children may find a permanent family through adoption. Whether it's short-term or long-term, fostering is always about what is best for the child at the time.

Just like Dottie, who is learning to be proud of her foster family, it is important to be kind and understanding to all children, whether they are in foster care or not. Dottie's friends showed her that there is no reason to feel ashamed, and they helped her to feel proud of her own, unique story. If you meet someone who is living with a foster family, treat them with the same kindness and respect as you would with anyone else, just like Dottie's friends did for her!

About the Author

Vicky Phillips is a Primary School Teacher with a passion for storytelling. She has spent many joyful years working with children and it is often the little things that they say or do that spark new ideas for her stories. Vicky especially enjoys sharing rhyming picture books with those she teaches, watching how the rhythm and wordplay can light up a child's imagination.

Vicky began writing while working for a teaching resource company, where she created comprehension texts for young readers. Although she enjoyed writing both fiction and non-fiction texts, it was the short, imaginative tales – with playful characters and thoughtful messages – that she found most rewarding and creatively fulfilling.

More recently, Vicky has begun a new chapter in her writing journey by creating a number of picture books. These stories are inspired by the curiosity and playful cheekiness that she sees in her classroom every day. With each book, she hopes to bring smiles to young readers' faces, while gently sharing lessons that children can carry with them.

First published in paperback in 2025 by
Michael Terence Publishing
www.mtp.agency

ISBN 9781805880035

Illustrated by
Shey Kolee

Michael Terence
Publishing

Printed in Great Britain
by Amazon

60959752R00020